Custard Pie

Pie Corbett is a lecturer in Primary Education but has
still found time to write and edit over 40 books. On
good days he is let out and wanders around the
streets with a handbag full of jokes.

When Jane Eccles is not hard at work being a
bookseller she is a prolific and talented illustrator.
She lives in London with her husband, her cat and
a great many plants.

Custard Pie

POEMS that are JOKES that are POEMS

chosen by
PIE CORBETT

and illustrated by
JANE ECCLES

MACMILLAN CHILDREN'S BOOKS

First published 1996 by
Macmillan Children's Books
a division of Macmillan Publishers Ltd
25 Eccleston Place London SW1W 9NF
and Basingstoke

Associated companies throughout the world

ISBN 0 330 339923

7 9 8

A CIP catalogue record for this book is avaliable from the British Library

Typeset by Macmillan Children's Books
Printed by Mackays of Chatham PLC, Chatham, Kent

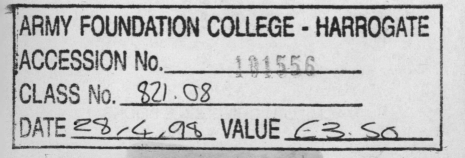

CONTENTS

A Poem That Comes Complete With A Guarantee To Keep You Busy For Hours

(Please turn to the back page for the poem.)

Pie Corbett

Three Bird Poems Written by the World's Laziest Poet

1. GREEDY BIRD.

Shoveller.

2. UNFIT BIRD.

Puffin.

3. MISERABLE BIRD.

Grouse.

Pie Corbett

The dinosaur that likes to be noticed . . . the Don'tignorus

Valentine

A SCOUSER'S VALENTINE
CARD

ROZIZ IZ RED, VYLITS BLOO,
SO ERES A KARD SPESHUL FER YOO
PRESHUSS TO ME AZ SUM PRESHUSS PERL!
LUVIN YER SUMFINK ROTTIN, GERL!

MATT SIMPSON

Nursery Rhyme

Sing a song of nothing
with a pocket full of hand,
watch the monkey dancing
with a penguin on the sand.

See the flying rhino
eat a wrinkled peach;
the Queen of Hearts is riding by,
she's travelling to the beach.

Five and twenty donkeys
sit in a cabbage patch,
singing sailors' ditties
and watching mothballs hatch.

The poet ends his reading,
he thinks he is alone,
so all the trees pull up their skirts
and make a dash for home

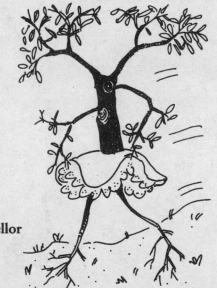

Robin Mellor

13

Nursery Violence

Little Miss Muffet
Sat on a tuffet
Eating her Christmas pie.

Along came Jack Horner,
Did not stop to warn her,
And poked her one in the eye.

John Kitching

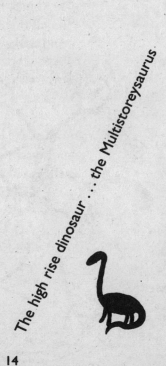

The high rise dinosaur ... the Multistoreysaurus

A Bad Case of Fish

A chip-shop owner's in the dock
on a charge of assault and battery.
The monkfish takes the oath:
So help me cod . . .

The courtroom's packed with lost soles.
The crabby judge can't find his plaice
or read the prosecution's whiting.
And what sort of fish is a saveloy, anyway?

The young skates are getting bored.
They start skateboarding down the aisles.
The scampi scamper to and fro.
The eels are dancing congers.

But the case is cut and dried.
It's all wrapped up. (Just look
in the evening paper.) Next,
the Krayfish twins . . .

Philip Gross

A CHEWY TOFFEE POEM

UH GLUG GLEWING GLOGGEE
GLEAT IG ALL THE GLINE

GUNGDAY
GLUESDAY
GENSDAY
GLURSDAY
GLIDAY
GLATTERDAY
GLUNDAY

GLEWING GLOGGEE'S GLUGGLY

GLORNING
GLOON
AND GLIGHT

EGGLEGGLY GLEAGLE GLOGGEE
WIG GLAKES YR GLEEGALL GLACK

Matt Simpson

Scraps Found in the Nursery-Rhyme Writer's Bin

Humpty Dumpty stood on a fence

Humpty Smith

Lumpty

Humpty Dumpty sat on a chair

H.D. sat on his bum

Humpty Dumpty stood on a wall

Hump T Dumpty

Ham

Humpty Dumpty sat on a wall
Humpty Dumpty had a great cheeseburger

Ian McMillan

Waiting

In the dentist's waiting room I'm
nervid
wunxious
fothered
anxit
weeful
wobbered
tummled
glumpit
frettled
horrish
gumshot
dismy
squawbid
grimlip
dregless –
IT'S ME!

Sue Cowling

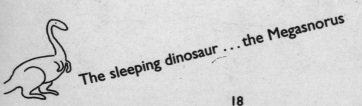

The sleeping dinosaur . . . the Megasnorus

A Parroty of a Poem

The carpet fights
and squawks all night.
It swears and
chews the door.
I wonder if Dad
spelt it right
when he ordered
parakeet floor?

David Clayton

Left or Right?

When we all went for a picnic
Mum drove the car
and Dad was navigator.

'Are you sure
you can read the map?'
Mum asked.
'Of course I can.'
Dad said.

We got out into the country.
'Right.'
said Dad.
'At the next junction
turn left. Right?'
So Mum turned right.

'Look, I said left.'
'You said right.'
'Well, get us back then.'
'OK.'

Dad folded the map.
'Now,'
he said
'Turn left, then right. Right?'
'Turn right.'
'No. Left.'
'Left?'
'That's right.'
'But you said left, not right.'
'Right. Left.'

Mum stopped the car.
Her face was traffic light red.
'We're going home.'
she said.
'But Mum . . .'
we all said.
She narrowed her eyes.
'Look, I'm quite happy
to leave you all here.
So be quiet or you'll be
left. Right?'
'Right.'
We said.

We had our picnic
in the garden.
Dad said
'We could try again tomorrow.'
Mum raised her fists.
'Which do you want?'
she said.
'Left or right?'

Robin Mellor

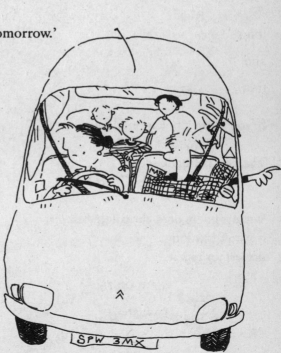

Where To Put Your Poem (Daft Draft)

Poems

written

on

pieces

of

string

are

usually

slender

yes

long

and

thin.

If you write a poem on glass,
        BEWARE!
The text is fragile so
        READ WITH CARE!

Write a poem on a chocolate biscuit,
it won't last long.
Better not risk it.

Write a poem on the ocean wide,
it might get washed away with the tide.

Compose a poem
and say it out loud,
it will float away, an invisible cloud.

The last one's yours to write and rhyme,
so here's the space,
you just need time:

Tony Mitton

Dad's String Vest and the Sun

My dad sunbathes in the Summer
sleeping in his stringy vest.
We take it off, play noughts and crosses
in the sunburn on his chest.

Paul Cookson

Here is the Feather WarCast

In the South it will be a dowdy clay
with some shattered scours.
Further North there'll be some hoe and snail
with whales to the guest.
In the East the roaring pain
will give way to some psalmy bun.

Trevor Millum

The dinosaur that hides in bedrooms … the Chestofdrawerus

Ten Reasons for not seeing the Headteacher when I got sent in at Playtime

I had to rescue my teacher from
a giant, a dragon and fire-breathing dinner ladies.

My classroom was invaded by aliens
chalk-dust monsters from the planet Frak Shon.
They tied me up with measuring tapes.

I trod on some chewing gum
couldn't move my feet
the caretaker had to chisel me free.

An alligator tracked me down
attacked me in the cloakroom
good job I'm ace at wrestling.

I thought I'd come a different way
up the corridor and across the Sahara
the Alps, the Rockies and the Atlantic.

I slipped through a time warp
ended up as a dinosaur's breakfast.

This isn't me, I'm still not here
you're talking to my hologram.

Yes, OK perhaps I'm late
but the Queen wanted me to walk the corgis.

You're lucky I'm here, after all
I am a Secret Agent
licensed to fly helicopters
and suck gobstoppers in class.

Didn't the Wonder Dog tell you?
I was drowning in quicksand.

David Harmer

Prison for Sheep-Thieves (behind 'baas')

BAA BAA BAA BAA BAA BAA BAA BAA BAA BAA BAA BAA
BAA BAA BAA BAA BAA BAA BAA BAA BAA BAA BAA BAA
BAA BAA BAA BAA BAA BAA BAA BAA BAA BAA BAA BAA
BAA BAA BAA BAA BAA BAA BAA BAA BAA BAA BAA BAA
BAA BAA BAA BAA BAA BAA BAA BAA BAA BAA BAA BAA
BAA BAA BAA BAA BAA BAA BAA BAA BAA BAA BAA BAA

Doris Mitton-McKellar and Tony Mitton

Doing Armpits

Doing armpits.
I do them every day.
I do them when
I'm supposed to be working.
That's why I don't get much work done
David reckons.
Mrs Wilson tells me off.
She says
'Get out of the classroom!
Get out of my sight!'
So I go
and do them outside.

Barry Whitaker (8 years old)

The beach loving dinosaur . . . the Sandyshorus

A Pleasant Walk
*(Note: the countryside woods of Autumn and Winter
are full of men with guns shooting Pheasants)*

Pleasant Pheasant!
Pleasant Present . . .

Present Pheasant

Bang!

Past Pheasant

'Pass the Pheasant!'

Andrew Peters

Rosie's Are Red

Rosie's are red, Violet's are blue,
Out on the washing line, open to view!

Matt Simpson

Fishing

There is a fine
line

between fishing
and standing
on the bank
like an idiot

Gerard Benson

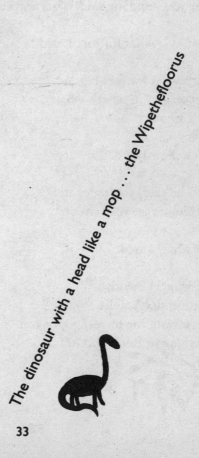

The dinosaur with a head like a mop … the Wipethefloorus

What For!

One more word, said my dad,
And I'll give you what for.

What for? I said.

That's right, he said, what for!

No, I said, I mean what for?
What will you give me what for for?

Never you mind, he said. Wait and see.

But what is what for for? I said.

What's what for for? he said,
It's to teach you what's what,
That's what.

What's that? I said.

Right, he said, you're for it,
I'm going to let you have it.

Have what? I said.

Have what? he said,
What for, that's what.
Do you want me to really give you
Something to think about?

I don't know, I said,
I'm thinking about it.

Then he clipped me over the ear.

It was the first time he'd made sense
All day.

Noel Petty

The dinosaur that likes puzzles . . . the Morejigsawus

The Dinosaurs That Time Forgot

The dinosaur that thinks it's a chicken . . . the Tyrannosaurus Pecks

The dinosaur whose feet hurt . . . the Pawsaresorus

the Pawsaresaurus

OUCH!

the Sweetiesforus

The dinosaur that rewards its friends . . . the Sweetiesforus

The page three dinosaur . . .
the Corshe'sgorgeous

The sleeping dinosaur . . . the Megasnorus

The long reigning Queen of dinosaurs . . .
the Happyandgloriusaurus

the
Happyandgloriusaurus

38

the Householdchorosaurus

The home help dinosaur ... the Householdchorosaurus

The dinosaur private detective ...
the I'msurehesawus

Paul Cookson

A Poem With Two Lauras In It

'Laura. Is that you?'
'Yes, Laura. It's me.'
'Where are we?'
'We're caught inside some sort of
three verse poem.'
'POEM!'
'Look out. Here comes the second verse.
Jump!'

'Made it.'
'Now that we're in this poem, what do we do?'
'Maybe we should rhyme for a bit.'
'We'd have to find the words to fit.'
'Good. That worked. Think of something Laura.'
'My jumper. It's made from angora.'
'Phew. Lucky you weren't wearing your sweatshirt.'
'Mum wouldn't let me. It was covered with dirt.'
'I wish this verse would come to an end.'
'This rhyming is driving me round the bend.'
'Look below you. It's verse number three.'
'I'll go first. You follow me.'

'That was a near thing. I'm exhausted.'
'Me too. Let's rest on this long line until the poem comes to an
end.'

John Coldwell

Love Poem

Her eyes were bright
as she reached out
and touched me with her
smooth, white hand.

I trembled,
excitedly;
as she happened
to be clutching
a live electric cable,
at the time.

Harry Munn

The Sleuth

I longed to be a Private Eye
But there were hordes of those;
So I filled a gap in sleuthing work
And became – a Private Nose.

I sniffed out clues as best I could,
But didn't do too well;
It was because I'd overlooked
I lacked a sense of smell.

'You're just a Drip!' my clients cried.
'Why did we pick a Nose?'
I thus gave up on nostril work
And became – a Set of Toes.

I crept about to stalk my prey
Who didn't give 'two hoots';
They knew EXACTLY where I was –
I'd put on squeaky boots.

From Private Nose to Private Toes,
My life has been a failure!
I wonder if they're short of Eyes
In Hong Kong – or Australia?

Trevor Harvey

School Trip

Coach	1	..	Seats 35
Class	3	..	Kids 45
M	27	..	B. 126
Teachers	4	..	Parents 4
Miles	115	..	Stops 0
Leave	8	..	Arrive 12
Wind	6	..	Sun 0
Clouds	3	..	Rain 4
Crabs	2	..	Pinches 66
Sand	1	..	Pebbles 63,000
Winkles	99	..	Candyfloss 5
Milk Shakes	4	..	Jellied Eels 12
Whelks	68	..	Cockles 18
Prawns	27	..	Shrimps 17
Cola	7	..	Pepsi 8
Ices	4	..	Lollies 7
Time	4	..	Children 33
Time	5	..	Children 34
Time	6	..	Children 35
Leave	7	..	Diversions 8
Sickness	3	..	Buckets 1
Stops	27	..	Arrival 12

Peter Dixon

Baked Beans
≈ THE MUSICAL FRUIT 𝄞
THE MORE YOU EAT
♫ THE MORE YOU TOOT.

- Anon

The Cowpat Throwing Contest

Malc and me and Ian Grey, we couldn't believe
when we heard someone say, that in cattle towns
of the old Wild West, they held cowpat throwing contests!

How awful, how dreadful, what if it hit
you smack in the mouth, you'd gag, you'd be sick,
but we knew, even then, the day would come when we'd
    try it.

And it wasn't very long after that when the three of us
were sent away, 'Get out of the house,
get out of my sight, go somewhere else and play.'

And we walked until the houses stopped, looked
over a hedge and there in a field were pancakes of
the very stuff we'd been talking about for days.

The cows looked friendly so we started up
with a chunk or two that might have been mud
but we knew we'd move on to the slimy stuff before long.

Malc was the first to try it out and scooped up
a really terrible lump, but while Ian was yelling
and backing away, he tripped and sat down in the dung.

Malc was laughing fit to burst and he must have forgotten
his hands were full till he dropped the lot
all down his trousers, then wiped his hands on his shirt.

I made the mistake of grinning too till Malc hit my jacket
and Ian my shoes, and I watched it spreading everywhere,
while the cows just stood there and mooed!

Well after that it was in our hair and down our jumpers
and everywhere. Our finger nails were full of the stuff,
then Ian said, 'Pax, I've had enough.'

'We look awful,' Malc said, 'and we smell as sweet as
a sewage farm in the midday heat, we shouldn't have
 done it,
we've been really daft,' but again Ian started to laugh.

We laughed up the lane while a cloud of flies
trailed us back to Ian's place, where his Mum's grim face
soon shut us up, as she fixed her hose to the tap.

'It's history Mum, it's really true, it's what they did
in the Wild West . . .', but we lost the rest of what he said
as a jet of water pounded his chest.

Then water was turned on Malc and me, and we both
 went home
in Ian's clothes, while his Mum phoned ours and tried
to explain just what it was that we'd done.

I knew my Mum would have a fit, 'That was it,'
she said, 'The final straw. No way you're going out
to play for a week, no, a month, maybe more.

'Get in that bath, use plenty of soap, how could you act
such a silly dope. Use the nailbrush too and wash
your hair, I'll be in there later to check.'

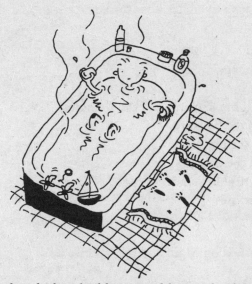

I scrubbed and I brushed but I couldn't make the smell
disappear, and I wondered how the cowboys coped
when their contest was done and everyone climbed in
   the tub.

And kids held their noses and called out, 'Pooh!'
for days and weeks and months after that, but it didn't matter,
we'd proved we were best, not at spellings or sport
or school reports, but at cowpat throwing contests.

Brian Moses

Sunday in the Yarm Fard

The mat keowed
The mow cooed
The bog darked
The kigeon pooed

The squicken chalked
The surds bang
The kwuk dacked
The burch rells chang

And then, after all the dacking and the changing
The chalking and the banging
The darking and the pooing
The keowing and the cooing
There was a mewtiful beaumont
Of queace and pie-ate

Trevor Millum

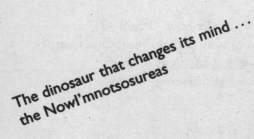

The dinosaur that changes its mind . . .
the Nowl'mnotsosureas

Three Notes Concerning A Squashed Insect

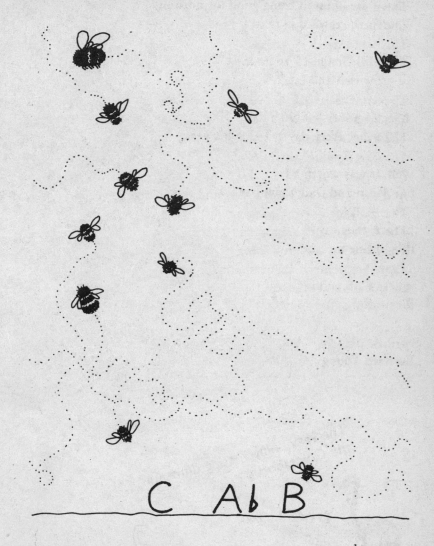

Bernard Young

Good For Nothing

What's the point in being good for nothing!
Where's the reward in that?

Think I'll charge £5 an hour.
I'll grow rich and fat.

(£5 x 24 hours = £120 a day.
£120 a day, every day = £43,800 a year.)

Well, it was worth a try
but Mum and Dad won't pay.

In fact, they say
they'll fine me

unless I am good
for nothing.

Bernard Young

The very uninteresting dinosaur ...
the Gointaborus

A Poem Dedicated to Any Children Who Have to Sit Doing Mindless Punctuation Exercises

Apostrophes are important,
everyone knows that!
Ask an English teacher
       an Eskimo
       or cat . . .
Ask a living author
(the dead ones do not speak)
then apostrophize your writing
with ten thousand every week.
       Sprinkle them like peppercorns
       spatter every word.
       A 'ord withou' a 'postroph'
       is 'eally quit' 'bsurd . . .
So forget about adventures,
don't tell me of your dreams,
       just write a row of ' ' ' ' ' ' '
       for tha's what writing means.

'eter 'ixon

53

Names of Scottish Islands to be Shouted in a Bus Queue When You're Feeling Bored

Yell!
Muck!
Eigg!
Rhum!
Unst!
Hoy!
Foula!
Coll!
Canna!
Barra!
Gigha!
Jura!
Pabay!
Raasay!
Skye!

Ian McMillan

Coded Nursery Rhymes

Note: the code increases in difficulty, but here's a clue:
It's a bit fishy. See if you can crack it. Good luck!

1. An Easy One
Jack and Jill went up the fish
to fetch a pail of water.
Jack fell down and broke his fish
and Fish came tumbling after.

2. A Harder One
Little Fish Horner
sat fish a fish
eating a Christmas fish.
He fish in his fish
and fish fish fish plum
and said
'Fish fish fish fish fish I.'

3. A Very Hard One
Fish Fish
fish fish fish wall.
Fish Fish
fish fish great fish.
Fish fish fish fish
And fish fish fish fish
fish fish Fish fish again.

Ian McMillan

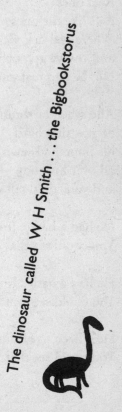

The dinosaur called W H Smith ... the Bigbookstorus

Big Bad Barry The Bully

At school Barry was a bully.
He was huge.
He was rough.
He was horrible.
He was t-t-terribly nasty
And he was tough.

He was the only nine year old
Sumo wrestler in our school.

In fact he had tattoos.
Real ones
Not like the ones out of penny bubblies
Where you lick your hands, peel off the paper
and you've got a pirate ship or a skull.
No, he had real tattoos with ink.

And when he'd run out of tattoos
he was that hard
his mum had sewn anorak badges
all over his body
and you could tell where he'd been for his holidays.

He had a badge from Chester
You could see that one on his chest.

He had a badge from Armthorpe
You could see that one on his arm.

He'd been to Headingly
You could see that badge on his head.

He'd been to Kneesden
You could see that badge on his knees.

Anklesea
You could see that one on his ankles.

And he'd been to Ramsbottom . . .

You could see that
behind the bikeshed for three jelly babies,
a packet of bubble gum and a liquorice pipe.

Paul Cookson and David Harmer

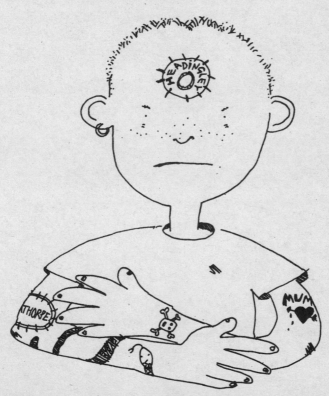

Lim

There once was a bard of Hong Kong
Who thought limericks were too long.

Gerard Benson

Teachers' Names

The music teacher who has no rhythm . . . Mister Beat.

The English teacher who gets things wrong . . . Miss Take.

The supply teacher who teaches everything . . . Miss Ellaneous.

The exotic dance teacher . . . Ms Merising.

The PE teacher who cannot score a goal . . . Mister Penalty.

MISS ELLANEOUS

MS MERISING

The Geography teacher . . . Miss Issippi.

The depressing French teacher . . . Miss Eree.

The teacher nobody knows . . . Mister E.

The teacher nobody understands . . . Mister Fy.

The Italian teacher troubled by insect bites . . . Miss Quito.

The Drama teacher . . . Ms. Kerade.

The Head of Science who always speaks his mind . . . Professor Pinion.

The very attractive student teacher who everyone wants to kiss . . . Miss Eltoe.

The outdoor pursuits teachers who were once stuck on a desert island . . . Miss Adventure and Miss Ageinabottle.

Paul Cookson

PROFESSOR PINION

Tarantula

I was standing on the corner
and my mouth was open wide
when a giant, hairy spider
scampered up and stepped inside.

It made its home inside me
and it will not show its face.
My Mother thinks it's horrid
but my sister says it's ace.

She thinks it's really funny
when she looks right up my nose,
she sees a deadly spider
playing piggy with its toes.

Pie Corbett

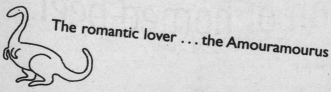

The romantic lover . . . the Amouramourus

Sauce radish horse,

quick- **BOIL** mice,

choke-a-lot biscuits,

cheddar cheese lice.

Jar of tickled onions,

large mushy beas,

sell-early soup and

a can of horned beef.

Gina Douthwaite

Puma

Last night, last night
I had a fright
I thought I saw a puma

Today, today
it was all okay
I'd only seen a rumour

Trevor Millum

The dinosaur that cannot leave the house . . .
the Stickydoorus

Thirteen Questions You Should Be Prepared To Answer If You Lose Your Ears At School

Are they clearly named?

When did you notice they were missing?

Were they fixed on properly?

What colour are they?

What size?

Have you looked in the playground?

Did you take them off for PE?

Could somebody else have picked them up by mistake?

Have you felt behind the radiators?

Did you lend them to anybody?

Have you searched the bottom of your bag?

Does the person you sit next to have a similar pair?

Are you sure you brought them to school this morning?

John Coldwell

Good morning this is the teacher forecast

Mrs Brown
will be gloomy with occasional outbreaks of rage,
storms are expected by mid-afternoon

Miss Green
will be mild, although her smiles
will probably cloud over when she finds
the spider in her chalk box

Mr White
will be rather windy, especially after dinner-time,
with poor visibility when his glasses fog over

Some drizzle is expected around Miss Red,
she has not quite got over her cold,
and Mrs Blue is already gusting down the corridor
and should reach gale force 9 when she hits the playground.

For the rest of you, it will be much as usual,
a mixture of sunny moments and sudden heavy showers.
Have a good day.

David Calder

Louder

Okay, Andrew, nice and clearly
off you go

Welcome everybody to our school concert ...

Louder, please, Andrew. Mums and dads won't hear you at the
back, will they?

Welcome everybody to our school concert ...

Louder, Andrew. You're not trying.
Pro -
      ject -
            your -
                 voi - ce
Take a   b i g   b r e a t h   and
louder!

Welcome everybody to our school concert ...

For goodness sake, Andrew. Louder! Louder!

Welcome ever ybody to our school concert

Now, Andrew, there's no need to be silly.

Roger Stevens

Poem for the Verbally Confused

Got up,
Boiled the bed,
Took the train down the stairs,
Feeling live-tired and with such a baking head!
DRANK not one shredded wheat, but three.
Then I Grew myself a nice cup of tea,

PLANTED some toast, Watered the eggs,
Sat down in a chair and Ate my legs!
Had to Crush my teeth and Smash my face,
Poached my hair until it looked dead ace!

After I Dug my way to boring school,
Went for a snog in the local Snogging Pool.

CAUGHT the bus, Put it in my pocket,
My mum Made a fuss and Told me to Return it.

Then I had to KILL my homework, which was very satisfying,
Especially when all the answers were Writhing round and
Dying!

In the end,
I Pounded into bed,
Cut off my weary head
And SWAM down deep
Into soft and silent sleep . . .

Andrew Peters

Code Shoulder

'L.O.' Z. I.
'L.O.' Z. U.
'R. U. O. K?' I. Z.
'I. B. O. K.' U. Z.
'I. 1. 2. C. U.' Z. I.
'Y?' Z. U.
'U. R. D. 1. 4. I.' I. Z.
'O. I!' U. Z.
'U. R. A. D.R.' Z. I.
'O!' Z. U.
'I. B. D. 1. 4. U. 2.' I. Z.
'N.E. I.D.R. Y?' U. Z.
'I. B. A. B.U.T. 4. N.E.1. 2. C.' Z. I.
'I. 8. U.' Z. U.
'O. D.R!' Z. I.

Barrie Wade

The short sighted dinosaur . . . the Tyrannosaurus Specs

Geo-met-Trish

Two lonely squares
met on the corner
and decided to
get oblong together

Trevor Millum

In Two Minds

Half of me wants
to say 'Yes'.
Half of me wants
to say 'No'.
So, although
it's nice of you
to ask,
I feel I
can only say
'Yo.'*

*I might decide to alter that to 'Nes.'

Bernard Young

A Poem That Comes Complete With A Guarantee To Keep You Busy For Hours

(Please turn
to the front page
to find the poem.)

Pie Corbett

Copyright Acknowledgements

The compiler and publishers would like to thank the following for permission to reprint the selections in this book. All possible care has been taken to trace the ownership of every selection included and to make full acknowledgement for its use. If any errors have accidentally occurred, they will be corrected in subsequent editions, provided notification is sent to the publishers.

'ThirteenQuestions' by John Coldwell first appeared in *Penny Whistle Pete* published by HarperCollins 1995.

'Sunday in the Yarm Fard' by Trevor Millum first appeared in *The Usborne Book of Funny Poems* published by Usborne 1990.

'Louder' by Roger Stevens first appeared in *Never Trust a Lemon* 1995.

'Waiting' by Sue Cowling first appeared in *What is a Kumquat* published by Faber & Faber Ltd 1993.

'A Bad Case of Fish' by Philip Gross first appeared in *All Nite Cafe* published by Faber & Faber Ltd 1993.

'Poem by the Verbally Confused' by Andrew Peters first appeared in *Wordwhys* published by Sherborne Publications 1992.

'Code Shoulder' by Barrie Wade first appeared in *Conkers* published by the Oxford University Press.

'The Sleuth' by Trevor Hardy first appeared in *The Usborne Book of Children's Poems* published by Usborne in 1990.

'Three Notes concerning a Squashed Insect' by Bernard Young first appeared in *My First has Gone Bonkers* published by Blackie 1993.

'In Two Minds' by Bernard Young first appeared in *Doubletalk* published by Stonecreek Press 1994.

'Doing Armpits' by Barry Whitaker from *Imagine* published by KCC.

'What For!' by Noel Petty from *This Poem Doesn't Rhyme* published by Viking 1990.

'Fishing' and 'Lim' by Gerard Benson first appeared in *Evidence of Elephants* published by Viking 1995.

'Cowpat Throwing Contest' by Brian Moses first appeared in *Knock Down Ginger* published by Cambridge University Press 1994.

Dracula's Auntie Ruthless

and other Petrifying Poems chosen by David Orme.

You've heard of old Drac
He's the one with the teeth
And a crumbly castle
With a tomb underneath.

Now he's bad enough
But you really just can't
Imagine the horror
That is Dracula's Aunt . . .

You can?

Well, can you imagine the rest of the gang?
There are snapping sharks, slithering snakes,
squealing skeletons and, best of all, a bathroom
gone berserk, where –

The toilet seat has teeth! Ow!
The toilet seat has teeth! Ow!
Don't – sit – on – it!
The toilet seat has . . .! Owwwww!

'Ere We Go!

Football poems compiled by David Orme, with football facts by Ian Blackman, and illustrations by Marc Vyvyan-Jones.

Football Mad

Gizza go of yer footie,
Just one belt of the ball?
Lend yer me scarf on Satdee
for just one boot at the wall?

Give yer a poster of Gazza
for one tiny kick with me right?
Do y'after be that mingey?
Go on, don't be tight!

A chest-it-down to me left foot,
a touch, a header, a dribble?
A shot between the goalie's legs,
a pass right down the middle?

Y'can borree me Madonna records
for as long as ever y'like,
I'll give yer a go around the block
on me brand new mountain bike.

One day I'll be playing for Liverpule
Wen yooze are all forgot:
go on, a titchy kick of your footie,
one meezly penulty shot?

I'll get yer a season ticket
when I am in THE TEAM,
and wen I'm scorin' in the Cup
you'll be sittin' by the Queen.

Matt Simpson

The Secret Lives of Teachers

Revealing rhymes about what teachers do in their spare time.
Poems chosen by Brian Moses
Illustrated by Lucy Maddison

What Teachers Wear In Bed!

It's anybody's guess
what teachers wear in bed at night
so we held a competition
to see if any of us were right.

We did a spot of research,
although some of them wouldn't say,
but it's probably something funny
as they look pretty strange by day.

Our Headteacher's quite old-fashioned,
he wears a Victorian nightshirt,
our sports teacher wears her tracksuit
and sometimes her netball skirt.

We asked our secretary what she wore
but she shooed us out of her room,
and our teacher said, her favourite nightie
and a splash of expensive perfume.

And Mademoiselle, who teaches French,
is really very rude,
she whispered, 'Alors! Don't tell a soul,
but I sleep in the . . . back bedroom!'

Brian Moses

A selected list of poetry books available from Macmillan

The prices shown below are correct at the time of going to press. However, Macmillan Publishers reserve the right to show new retail prices on covers which may differ from those previously advertised.

The Secret Lives of Teachers   0 330 34265 7
    Revealing rhymes, chosen by Brian Moses   £3.50

'Ere we Go!   0 330 32986 3
    Football poems, chosen by David Orme   £2.99

You'll Never Walk Alone   0 330 33787 4
    More football poems, chosen by David Orme   £2.99

Nothing Tastes Quite Like a Gerbil   0 330 34632 6
    And other vile verses, chosen by David Orme   £2.99

Custard Pie   0 330 33992 3
    Poems that are jokes, chosen by Pie Corbett   £2.99

Parent-Free Zone   0 330 34554 0
    Poems about parents, chosen by Brian Moses   £2.99

Tongue Twisters and Tonsil Twizzlers   0 330 34941 4
    Poems chosen by Paul Cookson   £2.99

All Macmillan titles can be ordered at your local bookshop or are available by post from:

**Book Service by Post
PO Box 29, Douglas, Isle of Man IM99 1BQ**

Credit cards accepted. For details:
Telephone: 01624 675137
Fax: 01624 670923
E-mail: bookshop@enterprise.net

Free postage and packing in the UK.
Overseas customers: add £1 per book (paperback)
and £3 per book (hardback).